MECHANICS OF THE HEART:

A COLLECTION OF SHORT STORIES ON LOVE, BETRAYAL AND RECUPERATION...

Presented by:
Lezlie Turner

www.pennedperfect.com
Instagram: @_xoxonae
Twitter: @_xoxoNAE

Acknowledgements

If you're reading this, you have either purchased my book or borrowed it from someone who did..... Either way, it means that I have achieved my goal and I am now an author! Yay!!! This accomplishment means so much to me and I truly appreciate all of your support. I hope you enjoy this book and I would love to hear your feedback. Thanks again for your support and please stay tuned because there is so much more to come!

Sincerely,
Lezlie S. Turner

Chapter 1 - (intro)

I was so naïve, I didn't know any better.
My friends tried to warn me, before we even got together.
I brushed them off. I told them we couldn't always have sunny skies.
There's nothing wrong, with a little stormy weather.
In all honesty, I think it may even make us better.
I tried to deal with all the hell you took me through, after all, isn't that what true lovers do?
Time after time, I kept my cool.
Now I've realized I... Played the Fool

Chapter 1

"He's no good for you! You deserve better, why can't you see that, Jade?" Those words were often preached to me. It was like hearing a broken record!

From the moment I met Tremaine, negativity has filled my ear. All I've heard was how he's no good, how he's playing me and how I deserved better. It seemed as if everyone and their mama had their opinion on why we shouldn't be together. Even though I knew everyone only wanted what's best for me, I wish they would keep their opinions to themselves.

What everyone couldn't seem to understand was that I loved him! Perfection is non-existent; they can't expect Tremaine to be perfect, neither can they expect our relationship to be perfect. Sure, he's in between jobs right now, he's cheated on me twice and has outside twins to show for it. However, that does not mean he does not love me back. Everybody makes mistakes! I wish people would just give him a fair chance.

I'm no *Perfect Patsy* myself, but there are no secrets between us. We have discussed every problem and fought to find a solution to overcome every obstacle we've faced. I have forgiven him and he has forgiven me. Deep down, I know Tremaine never meant to hurt me and as soon as he finds the time, he would find a stable job and start helping me with the bills.

Tremaine and I both planned to start saving money so we can move out of our small apartment and into a nice home and eventually, get married so we can start a family of our own. All I had to do was finish medical school and continue to cover my extra shifts at County General until he got on his feet. After that, everything should fall into place. Regardless of our issues, I'm going to continue to hold him down by any means necessary.

I could care less about what anyone has to say about our situation. Yes, I pay his child support and his kids stay with us from time-to-time. Yes, I buy his clothes, shoes, and keep him fed. All while paying the bills on my own, but I know in my heart, it's only temporary. I mean, Tremaine would do the same for me if I was in his position; so it was only right.

Just the other day my friend Jasmine was telling me how she seen Tremaine at the bar with his friends the night before last, acting as if he were single. She claimed that he was all up on some girl and that they even exchanged numbers. Supposedly Tremaine didn't see Jasmine until he was leaving and she confronted him and asked him about all of his flirtatious behavior. She said Tremaine referred to it as *harmless fun*. She went on to warn Tremaine that she was going to tell me about what she saw and she claims he responded by saying, "Jade will never believe you, she knows I don't club anymore."

The thing is, I do believe him. When he tells me that he is faithful and that the cheating and lying is all a thing of the past, I trust it. Jasmine is my girl and I know that she is only trying to look out for me, but I trust my man. The night that she claimed to have seen him is the same night that he was out of town assisting his cousin with a delivery. I'm sure Tremaine didn't pass up an opportunity to make money just to go to a bar! Besides that, the kids were home with me that night and he never would have left them if he did not have to go to work; he loves his babies. Maybe Jasmine mistook him for someone else.

I'm really not going to bother confronting him about that little situation, because like I said, I trust him and I know better. Jasmine thinks Tremaine is still the same old *Trey* from back in the day. She does not believe in second chances and thinks that I am dumb for giving him chance after chance to right all of his wrongs. Jasmine had seen me at my worst and has been there for me through all of it. She knows firsthand all the pain that Tremaine has caused me and she hates that I'm still with him after all that we've been through. My family also hates the fact that Tremaine and I are still together. Whenever he is around, they give him the cold shoulder. He has apologized to my family and even to Jasmine about the way that he has treated me in the past. He tries very hard to convince them that he deserves their forgiveness. I am praying hard for the day that they see him as I do. He's a great person, inside and out. Until then, we will just have to keep our distance. I have put a lot on the line for Tremaine these past three years and honestly, I have lost way more than I've gained. I still have faith that it's all going to be worth it in the long run though. That's what I keep telling myself. One day, all of this will make perfect sense.

* * * * * * * *

Six very long months have passed by and my prayers have finally been answered. Tremaine had found a permanent job with great pay and benefits. We have been saving money as planned and looking at houses as well. We plan to move within the next month or so. I am so happy and so blessed that things are finally looking up for us. Tremaine has also been throwing hints around about a ring, always asking about size and preference. That being said, I hear wedding bells!!!

Although things are going good right now, I do not want us to get ahead of ourselves. I learned at a very young age that high hopes only lead to disappointments, so I would rather us just follow our plans: job, house, and then marriage. So far, one down, two more to go. I'm in no rush at this point, I'm just going with the flow. Every day when Tremaine comes home from work, he has a gift for me. One day it may be a rose, the next day it may be a bear. It was just small sentiments to show me how much he appreciated me and everything that I have done for him.

He always says that he will never be able to repay me for all that I've done for him, but that one day he will come home with the best gift ever, and it will come pretty close. His words left me anxious. Especially since my birthday was coming up in a few months. Maybe I will get the mystery gift then. Seeing the change in Tremaine has brought me so much joy. I knew that he could do it and I am so glad that despite everyone's opinion, I never gave up on him.

Jasmine and I stopped speaking briefly when she told me about what she had seen at the bar. She said that she felt replaced when I believed Tremaine over her and that it would be best if we just distanced ourselves from one another. I tried to assure her that I was not trying to replace her or call her a liar or anything. I did not see it with my own eyes, therefore I did not want to cause trouble in my home because of it.

Although we have not spoken in a while, I called Jasmine up to invite her out for lunch; I wanted to update her on everything that has been going on lately. Hesitantly, she accepted my invitation and agreed to meet me at *Seven's*, one of our favorite seafood spots downtown. When Jasmine arrived, she could tell that I was happy. Immediately he said that I was glowing. I began to tell her how wonderful things have been going for Tremaine and I. She was not really saying much, just chowing down on her crab cakes; no response usually meant she didn't believe a word that I was saying.

After gobbling down two crab cakes and taking a sip of her drink, she finally responded. "I have heard this a million and one times Jade, but you have never been able to convince me that he isn't no good. However, it's obvious that you are happier than you were before, but I still don't trust him. All I'm going to say is that if you're happy, I'm happy for you."

Coming from Jasmine, that meant a lot and it gives me hope that in no time she will give Tremaine the chance he deserves.

* * * * * * * *

My birthday had finally arrived and I was so very anxious for Tremaine to get home from work. I had a good feeling that today would be the day that I would get that mystery gift. So far my day had been wonderful. I just found out that I aced my entrance exam and that I'd be starting my residency program in the fall. Proud to say that I'm officially Doctor Jade Johnson.

My mother took me to breakfast to celebrate and surprised me with a beautiful bracelet from Tiffany's. Jasmine took me to lunch on her break and surprised me with a super sexy birthday dress. The only thing I was missing now was Tremaine and his surprise.

While anxiously waiting, I dosed off to sleep and was awakened from my nap with a text from Tremaine. It read: *Get dressed baby I'm OMW, be there in an hour!* I jumped up in excitement. I showered, applied my smell good and put on my gift from Jasmine. I got myself dolled up super sexy for my boo.

Tremaine arrived right on time. He was all clean-cut, freshly dressed and handsome with roses and balloons in his hands. I figured he must've gotten off early and got dressed elsewhere, because he did not leave the house looking this way. I greeted him all giddy and childlike and thanked him for my balloons and roses. He responded with a kiss. He then told me that we needed to hurry up and leave before we ran late.

Tremaine opened the car door for me and I got inside and immediately began asking him questions. I was trying to figure out exactly where we were headed. He told me to just sit back, relax and enjoy the ride. I sat back, but I was still bursting with excitement.

After what seemed like the longest ride of my life, we finally stopped. Only problem was, I hadn't the slightest idea where we were. We are stopped in front of this gate that looked as though it led to a very long driveway. When the driveway stopped, a big beautiful house was before us. Tremaine hopped out of the car and ran over to open the door so that I could get out. I couldn't keep my eyes off this house.

As we reached the porch, I still had no idea where we were. Confused, I faced Tremaine. "Whose house is this?" I asked.

He smiled and handed me a small yellow box. I slowly opened it and found a key inside. Still confused, I looked up at his excited eyes.

"This house is yours, welcome home!" He smiled largely.

Shocked and amazed, I used the key to unlock the door. I was not at all expecting what awaited me behind it. My mother, my father, all of my siblings including Tremaine's mother and Jasmine were all inside. They held up a banner that read: *Happy Birthday Jade. Welcome Home!* I immediately burst into tears; happy tears of course. My home was everything I dreamed of and so much more; it was huge. Also, the people that I loved were all under one roof having fun and getting along, all for me.

Tremaine had dinner catered and we all enjoyed the fancy feast. My birthday couldn't get any better! I stopped at that thought when Tremaine announced that he had one more gift for me. I walked toward him with my hand over my chest because I was so surprised.

"After all of this, you mean to tell me you have another present?" I asked.

He laughed and handed me another yellow box. For some reason, I immediately thought it was a wedding ring. However, when I opened it, I discovered another key with a note that read: *follow me*. I looked puzzled at Tremaine as he got up from the table. He reached for my hand and led me to the garage.

Waiting for me in the garage was a very shiny black car. This wasn't just any car, it was a Benz! Just like the one I have always wanted. I was shocked! He promised that I would come home to the best gift ever given to me and that's exactly what happened. I gave him a look of gratitude. I planned to thank him for what he's done for me, every single day for the rest of my life. This birthday was truly one for the books. Jasmine even commended Tremaine on how well he had done to make this the best birthday ever.

The very next day, I woke up thinking it was all a dream. Everything still seemed so surreal. I had to keep reminding myself that I had really become a doctor, I was really living in my dream home and driving my dream car. Tremaine was really keeping his promises and doing right by me. The only thing that I struggled with, was the fact that Tremaine has yet to propose to me. I promised myself that I was not going to rush things, but it was all that I was missing. Everything had been going as planned and now, step three was marriage, and we are not even engaged!

Tremaine hadn't even mentioned a ring not one time since we moved into our new home. He recently got promoted and was working longer hours so he's hardly ever home for us to talk about this. I'm not even sure how he feels about us getting married now. I'm sure it is nothing to worry about though. He loves me, I love him, and we will be married soon enough.

During the past week, anxiety and doubt was starting to

take over me. At this point, I think marriage is never going to happen for Tremaine and I. He's still working long hours and coming home late. When he comes home, he just goes straight to bed without any talking, touching, or anything. He acts as if I'm not even there. It's all starting to stress me out. I can hardly concentrate on my residency because all I can think about is Tremaine.

I've been crying and worrying, scared to even ask him what the problem is because anytime I say something, we start arguing about my insecurities. I really wished I had someone to vent to, someone who would just listen to me. Honestly, I really needed Jasmine but a few days ago, we got into a huge fight.

The fight started when she tried to tell me that she heard that while I was thinking Tremaine was at work all this time, he was really with his baby mama. She said that word on the streets was that he moved her into our old apartment and spends the majority of his time there and then comes home to me when he feels like it. She said that the *job* Tremaine has, is really a cover up, and that he is a part of some big drug cartel. I couldn't believe she had the audacity to say that it explained how he got me all of these nice things for my birthday.

Jasmine knows damn well that I'm not a fan of *he said, she said, they said,* which is why she gathered so-called proof that she wanted to show me. I got angry and refused to look at it. I told her that I would ask Tremaine about it, but I will not accuse him of anything. She left my house enraged.

"I'm so sorry that you're so stupid and letting someone as trifling as Tremaine tear us apart!" I couldn't believe those words left her lips. Jasmine and I have been friends for six years. We had been through a whole lot together, but we have never had an argument like the one we had on Tuesday. I am almost positive that it was the end of our friendship.

I haven't spoken to my mother lately either. After she found out how much the stress of this relationship was affecting my residency, she suggested that I leave Tremaine alone and focus on me. That too caused a huge argument like never before. I ended up cursing my own mother out and because of that, my family can't even stand me right now. It really seems as if I'm losing myself. Every time I look in the mirror, I don't know who the person is looking back at me anymore. All I know, is that it's a must that I confront Tremaine when he comes home tonight. This cannot go on any longer.

I picked up my phone and sent him a text. *Come home now!! WE NEED TO TALK!*

As I expected, I got no reply. After four hours of nervously waiting, Tremaine finally walked through the door. When he approached our bedroom, I sat back against the headboard and immediately told him how I was feeling. I confronted him about all the rumors I had been hearing and I literally poured my soul out to this man.

"Stop overreacting baby, you trust me don't you?" Those were the only words he said to me. He took off his clothes and he showered and went to bed. That night I cried and I prayed. I prayed and I cried. I wanted God to reveal some things to me, I wanted him to take my pain away. I wanted to be set free and if that meant losing Tremaine, losing my dream home and even my residency, I wanted God to help me to be content with that. I was at my breaking point, I have had enough.

Tremaine and I slept in different rooms that night and when I woke up the next morning, he was gone. He took all of his belongings and left the house. He didn't even say goodbye, but he did leave a note. It read:

Jade,
I promised you that I would never lie to you again so here's the truth.

All of those rumors you heard, they are all true. I'm so sorry that I've hurt you.

Now I've decided to make it right, by leaving. I'm no good for you baby and you're too good for me. You deserve so much better and I hope you find it. Don't worry about anything, you can have the house and the car. I gave you those gifts out of love. If there's one thing I didn't lie about, was my love for you.

You are the best thing that ever happened to me and I will be forever indebted to you. Take care and I wish you the best Doc.

Love always,
Tremaine

My heart felt heavy. Reading that note gave me a really strange feeling. I was overwhelmed with so many mixed emotions and one of those emotions oddly enough, just happens to be *happy*. I guess itwas becauseI was so in love with him that I lost myself. I lost my friends and even my family. In the midst of losing, I also gained. Tremaine's letter was a true eye opener. I felt like my faith was restored and that I found myself. It was time that I learned to love myself and to also believe people when they show me their character the first time. Second chances are to be earned, not given. If someone truly deserves a second chance, then they'll go above and beyond to prove it to you. Love ain't supposed to hurt, don't be a fool because I played one, but not anymore.

Chapter 2 - (intro)

You showed me a love I never knew.
I thought I'd spend the rest of my life with you.
I thought you were the one, someone not like the rest.
I thought that maybe, just maybe, you had passed the test.
Boy was I wrong, they really are all the same.
I guess it was just... All a Part of the Game

Chapter 2

Today marks the tenth year that Devin and I have been married. We met on Valentine's Day and I guess Cupid was aiming right at us because it was love at first sight. I knew from the very moment I met him that he was everything I have ever wanted in a man. Devin is such a selfless person and that's what I love most about him. Devin's my King and I am his Queen and he constantly reminds me of that. He works very hard to protect and provide for our family. In the beginning, I was afraid to love him and even more afraid to let him love me. Devin showed me a love that I never knew, a love so real that it actually felt unreal.

Because of my past, I did not think anyone deserved to love me. Honestly I did not think I should be loved at all. I harbored so much anger and hurt from my previous relationship that it was hard for me to trust anyone or anything. I figured that Devin must really love me if he put up with me and all of my issues. I carried so much baggage over into this relationship and then into our marriage that it's literally a miracle that we even made it this far. Often times I would catch myself questioning his love for me. I mean, I have never witnessed true love and I'm not sure that this is it but it seems like God has finally answered my prayers. At the same time, it seems too good to be true. Devin tries so hard to prove to me that he is nothing like the guy that hurt me from my past.

When I am at my lowest, Devin does everything in his power to pick me up. I appreciate that man like no other and I never want to lose him. I pray that someday I will be able to completely forget my past and focus on the present with my King.

Together, Devin and I share two kids, twelve year old Princess Mia from a previous relationship of mine and six month old, Prince DJ. Even though Devin isn't Mia's biological father, he is definitely her *daddy*! He came into her life when she was only two years old and she has loved him ever since. The fact that he loved her as his own from the very start is one of the things that made me fall madly in love with him. He knew that in order to get to me, he must first love her. And he had no problem doing so. I swear he is everything I dreamed my husband to be and I feel as though I'm living a fairytale life. In no way am I saying that we are perfect, but if I could just get rid of my baggage, I think we would come pretty close.

You would think that after ten years of Devin being in my life, I would have let my guard down already, but it's not that easy for me. I have been scarred and I honestly don't think there is no coming back from that. I really needed to get it together before I lose the man that I love. I sometimes feel as though I am pushing him away, but he says he understands my feelings. He is so patient with me and I wish that I could be as good of a wife to him as he is a husband to me. I prayed to God asking him to heal my hurt. He sent me Devin and I want to be able to show God that I am thankful. He knows my heart which is why he sent me such a good man but I want to feel like I deserve the blessing that he has given to me. Devin suggested that I go to counseling but I'm not too thrilled about it, however, I will do whatever it takes to save my marriage.

My husband set up a date for counseling and it arrived

quickly. I was so nervous, I couldn't even sleep the night before. I always had trouble opening up to people and I cry at the drop of a dime. This appointment had me feeling anxious. I wondered how this counseling session was going to turn out.

Bracing myself as I prepared to walk into the office, I said a quick prayer to calm my nerves. I took a deep breath and once inside, I found that it was a rather cozy little office with a huge marble desk in the middle of the floor. There was a big white futon in one corner and a recliner in the other. Sitting at the desk was an African American woman with long beautiful hair and a warming smile. She got up from the desk to greet me.

"Hi, my name is Doctor Lexington Childs." Her smile seemed pleasant. Although she seemed like a nice woman, I was still on the fence about opening up to her. I sat on the couch and took a deep breath. I was preparing myself to open up and become vulnerable and I was really nervous.

In the beginning of the session we got to know each other. I guess it was her way of breaking the ice. She told me a little about herself and then I told her a little bit about me. She asked me a few questions about my marriage, kids, childhood, family, and so-on. When I answered a question, she would also answer mine. Like me, she was married, has kids and also a few trust issues in the beginning of her marriage. Unlike me, she had been married twice so she had an idea of what she was getting into the second time around.

As we continued to share our life stories with one another, we discovered that we really had a lot in common. Before we knew it, our hour session had gone by. Surprisingly, I was a little sad that the session was over. She concluded by telling me that next week, we would get into the meat of the session.

"Great, thank you for everything Doctor Childs, I am actually looking forward to coming back next week."

I left the session feeling like some weight was being lifted off my shoulders. Since she'd been in my shoes in the past, I felt confident that she'd actually feel where I was coming from. I'm sure Devin will be pleased to know how much I enjoyed counseling. I actually owe him an apology for overreacting when he suggested this because it was nothing like I thought it would be. Now that I was more open to the idea of counseling, there were a lot of things that I wanted to ask Doctor Childs. I could hardly wait for next Thursday.

I slept comfortably that night and it was now Friday which was one of my favorite days of the week. Friday for us was family night. Every Friday night Devin's family and my family would all come to our house for food, drinks and family fun. I loved how we all operated as one big family. Everybody always got along and there was no fussing, no fighting all fun.

I've always been a very family oriented person, I lived for family gatherings. Devin's family was not as big as mine so they have always been close all his life. In the midst of enjoying the family festivities, I pulled my mom to the side to tell her about my counseling, I figured she would love to know that I was trying to let go of my past and focus on my marriage which she had been telling me to do for years now.

"Mom, I took your advice and sought help for my issues. Devin signed me up for counseling."

She looked at me puzzled. "I'm not a fan of a *shrink*." She rolled her eyes. I was shocked because I thought she would consider this to be good news.

"Child, Devin didn't need to find you someone to talk to. Your knees ailing you?" Confused I answered, "No ma'am."

"That's what I thought. You know what to do when you have a problem!"

I guess what my mom was trying to say was, whatever problems that I had, could be fixed with prayer. I took a seat on the couch and took in what she was trying to tell me. She was right, however, there was nothing wrong with talking to someone who had been through what I had.

My mom walked over to where I was sitting on the couch. She told me that although she does not agree with counseling, she promised to support me. She never meddled in my marriage so whenever I came to her, she voiced her opinion, gave me advice, but she would never force it on me.

After everyone had gone, I cleaned the house and tucked the kids into bed. I said my prayers and climbed into bed with my husband. Immediately he began to ask me all kinds of question about counseling and about Doctor Childs. He was happy with what I told him about her and was so glad that I had no complaints about it. He was very pleased to know that I enjoyed it.

He cuddled up behind me in bed. "This lets me know that our future will be just like I envisioned."

I smiled and scoot my body closer to his. "Thank you for recommending this idea. I apologize for being so closed minded at first."

"No problem babe." He said before drifting off to sleep.

I slept so peacefully that night knowing I was waking up to the most amazing man in the entire world.

It was Saturday morning and a very busy day for me. I decided to get up early and cook so that my family could wake up to the lovely smell of bacon and delicious weekend breakfast. I cooked all of their favorites. DJ had a doctor's appointment at ten and Mia had her very first dance recital at noon.

Everyone ate, got dressed and we were out of the house to start our day. The first stop was the doctor's office. DJ's checkup went well and now we had to go pick up my mom and head over to Mia's recital. We are all so very excited about seeing Mia perform. She had been practicing so hard, though she was a little bit nervous. I smiled at her little face, I knew she would do well.

LEZLIE TURNER

Devin had to do a little work at the office so he was going to meet us at the recital. I kept checking my watch hoping he'd be able to make it on time. Mia would be devastated if he missed it. It was five minutes before show time and Devin was not around. I called the office and I got no answer. I called his assistant and she said the offices were not even supposed to be open today. I called and texted his cellphone, left messages and still no answer.

The recital had ended and my baby did a great job! When she realized her daddy didn't make it, she was so upset. He was supposed to greet her at the end with roses like he'd promised. Where was he? This was not like him; he would never disappoint Mia or miss the most important day of her life. I was really starting to worry because hours had passed and I had yet to hear from Devin. I called all of the places I thought he may be and nobody had seen him. His parents were at Mia's recital and they didn't know where he was either. If he was not at home, I guess I would have to just sit and wait.

I was pacing the floor at home worried about my husband. Finally, nine o'clock rolled around and in walked Devin. I was relieved to see him and I was so glad he was okay. I greeted him with a big hug and then a slap across the face because I wanted to know where the hell he had been all this time. He laughed and told me to calm down.

"I got caught up at the office."

I gave him a puzzled look. "I called the office and your assistant told me that the offices were not even open."

"That's because I didn't bother calling her in because it wasn't anything I couldn't handle on my own."

I looked at him like he was crazy. I really hoped he didn't think I was buying the bullshit he was trying to sell me.

"Mia was so upset that you missed her recital. Go apologize to her!" I demanded.

After Devin apologized, I made him sleep on the couch. Actually, that's where he ending up sleeping that night, and the following week as well.

I was so glad to see Thursday because I was definitely going to get Doctor Childs' intake on this. Devin kept telling me that I was overreacting. I wanted to know if she'd agree with him or not.

When I walked into her office, I got straight to the point because I was eager to hear her opinion.

She took off her glasses and looked me straight in the eyes. "I understand why you are so cautious, but I don't think you have anything to worry about. The fact that you have been making him sleep on the couch all of this time is a bit much. I recommend that the both of you come to my office first thing tomorrow morning."

I agreed with Doctor Childs and once she dismissed me for the day, I went to my mother's house and told her of all of the things that had been going on in my home. She was not too happy about it. She told me to get my house in order. I spent hours at my mom's house because I really didn't even want to see Devin. Remembering everything that I have been through in my past, I couldn't help but think that Devin was up to no good when he missed Mia's recital. I hated that I was thinking this way because he was such a good man. I never wanted my insecurities to ruin my marriage but my intuition has never failed me.

I swallowed my pride and went home to tell Devin about our early morning appointment with Doctor Childs. He told me that he was paying her to help me, because I was the one with the issues, not him. I didn't bother arguing back with him. If he was going to come, he comes, if he chooses not to, then oh well, another night on the couch.

Morning came and I took the kids to my mother's and I asked her to just give me a word of encouragement.

"Everything will be alright, just think positive." I gave my mom a hug and then headed off.

Before getting out of the car, I sat in the parking lot of Doctor Childs' office and said a quick prayer. I hoped to gain some type of understanding and peace from this visit. When I got out of the car, I noticed that Devin's car was also in the parking lot. I smiled because I was so glad he decided to come. I walked into Doctor Childs' office feeling better already.

I noticed Devin and Doctor Childs were already engaging in conversation when I entered the room. They must've been talking about me because I startled them and Devin was looking all wide-eyed. As soon as I sat down, she began the session.

"Devin and I had become acquainted while waiting for you. It seems as though you have a wonderful husband. You should be thankful after all you've been through to finally have someone such as Devin in your life."

She smirked. She was basically telling me everything I already knew or what I thought I knew until he missed Mia's recital. I wondered what about my husband that was making her all *team Devin.*

By the time the session ended, Devin and I had made up. I thanked Doctor Childs for her help and we left. Devin and I decided to leave the kids with my mom a little longer and spend some quality time together. He took me to a really nice restaurant downtown that overlooked the city.

During brunch, we discussed our issues and apologized to each other for everything. I promised him that I would continue to see Doctor Childs and work on myself and he promised to drop by some of the sessions as well.

"I am beginning to think you like Doctor Childs just a little too much," I said jokingly.

"It's all for the sake of our marriage." He laughed back.

While waiting for the waiter to bring our check, Devin

asked to be excused. While he was in the restroom, his phone buzzed indicating that he had a text message. I hesitated while watching it vibrate. I knew I shouldn't do it, but what's his is mine; he's my husband. I picked up his phone and read the message and I was not at all prepared for what I was about to read.

Hey babe! I know you said we weren't going to be able to meet tonight, but I think you'll be able to get away thanks to me. She trusts you now lol! Call me when you can XOXO Lexington☺.

My eyes grew wide and I immediately began scrolling through their previous conversations trying to hurry before he returned from the bathroom. I found out that they have been seeing each other for a while now. She is the one who recommended that I come see her so that she could make me think my intuition was just my insecurities getting the best of me. It was a way of covering up their fling.

After gathering all the proof I needed, I got up from the table and left the restaurant. I went home and packed all of my belongings *and* my kids belongings and moved to my mother's house. I'm sure Devin won't be completely clueless when he returned to the table and realize that I was gone. I left the message thread up so he wouldn't be too surprised. I also left a note on the mirror with my lipstick in what used to be our bedroom and also on the kid's mirror that said, *I hope she was worth it!*

I knew there was a reason that I could never let my guard down. I just hated that it took me ten years to find what that reason was with Devin. My heart is going to break when my kids ask *where's daddy*, but I am doing what I feel is best for all of us. It seems as though me and my poor Mia can't win for losing; but we will be okay. I won't keep DJ from his father but I won't allow him to be in my life anymore. If he cheats once, he will do it again, but he won't be cheating on *me*! I have to set an example for my daughter and being in an unhappy marriage is not my idea of a good example. I think I would rather show her that you can make it without a man and I don't want her to feel like she has to depend on anybody for anything. It is important that she knows where her help comes from. I intend to raise her as my mother raised me, independently.

Chapter 3 - (intro)

The way you make me feel is unexplainable,
Words couldn't describe how deep my feelings are, even if they searched
beyond the dictionary very far.
I'm tired of being unofficial, I wanna' make this real,
If only you could feel how I feel.
Put yourself in position, see things as I do,
None of that really matters though, all I want is you.
So if this is how you want it to stay,
*This is how we'll keep it, cause' you're my....****Best Kept Secret***

Chapter 3

Today marks two years since mine and Julius's love affair began. I must say it has been one hell of a ride thus far. Sneaking in and out of different hotels, taking random business trips to far away cities, clocking in early, clocking out late; if these walls could talk, ain't no telling what this office would say.

It all started when I got a job working as a secretary at a well-known law firm in my hometown. In walked this tall, dark, clean-cut handsome man that had a smile that could brighten up the darkest room. I was told to refer to him as Mr. Parker because he was the boss. At first I was a little intimidated by him. He came across to be a little arrogant and egotistical. Over time, the more I worked for him, the better I got to know him. I later found out that he was nothing like what I expected.

All week he was working on what he called the biggest case of his career and because of that, he put in long hours at the office. One afternoon as I was proceeding to end my shift, Mr. Parker asked me if I would stay overtime to help him out. Feeling honored that he asked me, a newbie on the job, I quickly said, "yes!"

Going into his office, I really had no idea what to expect. I mean, what did he want me to do exactly? The most I've done is take calls and book meetings.

He was sitting at his desk when I entered.

"Have a seat," he smiled. I guess he could see that I was nervous.

"Relax, it's not like I'm putting you on the stand," he joked. "I'm just trying to review my case from a juror's perspective." I sat and took notes and did as I was told. After about five hours, Mr. Parks decided to wrap up for the night. He thanked me for staying, and asked me if I would mind staying again tomorrow and maybe even the rest of the week if I had the time. I agreed. I went home and went straight to bed knowing that my tomorrow would resume bright and early and be as long as my today.

I worked countless hours of overtime for two weeks straight and I was exhausted.

Grateful that today was Friday, I went to work in a marvelous mood looking great on the outside even though I was drained on the inside Thank God for coffee and concealer. I got to my desk about to perform my daily duties when I noticed I had an email from Mr. Parks. *Meet me for brunch at 11:45am at the corner café.. need to talk about last night ;)*

Interrupted by my co-worker in mid-response, I quickly closed the email to see what she needed. At exactly 10:58 am, I clocked out and headed for the café anxious and unexcited at the same time because I was not looking forward to discussing our late night office escapade. I'm assuming that will be the subject, since the topic of his email was *about last night*. I didn't understand why we needed to talk about it. I mean, it's not like that was the first time he replaced the hundreds of files on his desk with my body. When I arrived at the café, Mr. Parks was already there and had ordered for the both of us. He was rudely chowing down on his meal already.

He told me that he spent most of his morning in court and I guess he was too hungry to wait for me. I sat down at the table, greeted him and took a sip of tea. Awkwardly, I glanced across the table giving him a *go ahead and talk* kind of look.

Following a weird smirk, he finally wiped his mouth and spoke. "Well…I won the case." I smiled but I knew that wasn't the main reason he invited me to brunch but I played it off anyway.

"Congrats." I forced a larger smile.

"Thanks. The past few weeks we've been getting to know each other pretty well. I think we should celebrate by going out of town. I have you to thank for helping me win the case as well. So let's go to New York; it's strictly business. I also want to promote you from secretary to my personal assistant and I'd like for you to be with me in New York to meet my new client." He winked.

Deep down I knew that this trip was going to be a bit more than business, but I've never been to New York and I was excited that I had just got promoted. *Why decline?* I thought to myself.

After brunch, we said our goodbyes. Still excited about my trip, I could hardly wait to finish the work day so I could go home and pack. I zoned out so many times at my desk thinking about how fun New York was going to be that I almost missed several phone calls. As soon as my shift ended I hurried home to pack because our flight was leaving at 10:00 pm that same day.

It was almost six o'clock and I rushed around the house to get things together because Mr. Parker was picking me up at eight. After quickly packing I decided to take a quick power nap. I then woke up to the sound of a honking horn and a ringing doorbell. I grabbed my things and hurried to the door assuming it was Mr. Parker since I had three missed calls from him but I had no idea who the man in the suit was standing on my doorstep.

"Come, Madame," he said, taking my bags. "Your ride awaits you."

Mr. Parker must've seen the confused look on my face because he rolled his window down and waved. After seeing him, I proceeded to the very shiny, nice and black, deep tinted Escalade that sat in my driveway. I sat inside of the car next to Mr. Parker who was waiting in the backseat all dressed up in a suit and tie. "Pretty formal for a business trip." I took a deep breath. "Mr. Parker, couldn't we have just taken your car to the airport?" I asked.

"Please call me Julius, and you call this formal? This is my every day transportation darling." He smiled.

"Oh really? I never noticed, but anyway, thanks so much for inviting me Julius." I said as I got comfortable in my seat.

"No need for the thanks; it's part of your job now, remember?" He confirmed.

We rode in silence to the airport and when we arrived there, we boarded the plane and we were seated in first class. After a few hours or so, we landed in New York safely. Another Escalade picked us up and we were escorted to one of the nicest hotels I had ever seen!

At check-in, all he said to the receptionist was, "Julius Parker," and we were quickly escorted to the sixth floor where the hostess opened the door to what looked like it could be Heaven. The suite was so beautiful, I could hardly find the words to describe it. It was just breathtaking! Big beautiful crystal chandeliers hung from the ceilings, huge California King beds with silk sheets and a mattress softer than a baby's bottom filled the two spacious bedrooms. There was a nice garden tub in the master bath with our very own flat screen TV inside. In the entryway, there was a cozy sitting area that led to the kitchen, and the eating area looked like it could be inside of a Home Magazine. This suite was nicer than my entire house!

Julius could tell I was in awe because he was smiling as if he had done something great. It was late so instead of going out, we ordered room service and dined in. Julius promised to take me sightseeing in the morning. Although I was excited to be in New York, I didn't mind waiting till morning for our tour because I was pooped!

I rested well that night and was awakened in the morning by the smell of a delicious breakfast that I assumed Julius ordered for us. When we began to eat, the food was just as delicious as the smell of it. I gobbled it down as if I hadn't eaten in weeks.

After breakfast, I showered and got prepared for the day. I was super excited about the adventure that awaited me! Julius had a whole tour laid out for us. We jumped in the car and headed out. Upon arrival, were greeted by a very nice tour guide named Bronco who took us to see The Statue of Liberty, The Apollo Theater, a couple of famous neighborhoods, and even to where 9/11 happened.

After our tour, we had dinner at a place called *Mac's* where we enjoyed a nice dinner and a live show. Following dinner, we headed back to the hotel because we were pooped. It had been a long day for us and I just wanted to shower and sleep. As I was showering, I began humming and singing when I was startled by the shower door opening. I turned around to see Julius climbing in. Before I could say or do anything, he grabbed my naked body and one thing led to another.

Hesitantly, but willingly, I gasped as his body touched mine. I wasn't even sure of what was exactly happening but I let his love fill mine repeatedly. Still speechless after the shower, I climbed into bed and slept softly in his arms. Before I could even began to dream, it seemed like the alarm went off. It was time to say adios to New York and catch our flight back.

As we were preparing for takeoff, I turned to Julius because it seemed like we hardly handled any business on this trip.

"Julius, what happened to your client that we were supposed to be meeting?"

He grinned, "I had a terrific time with *her* on this trip. You were the 'client'. I just told you we were meeting someone because I didn't think you would've came otherwise."

I shifted back in my seat. He was probably right. If I knew that this trip had nothing to do with business, I would've probably declined. When we got back, we spent the remainder of that weekend together and even arrived to work together on Monday. After that trip, this had become a routine of ours. Taking business trips, carpooling and spending a lot of time together. Although we were happy and I guess you could even say we were in love, we decided to be discreet at work and not let the people at the office know about us.

Julius felt like it would cause drama for us to let anyone in the office know about our relationship. He especially felt like it would be drama for me and I certainly didn't want that. I didn't want anyone to think that there were any handouts given to me because of our relationship. It's completely not true because I worked hard. Maybe partly, but not completely. I understood how he felt so I agreed to remain discreet but of course that didn't stop people from making speculations. Every time a rumor circulated, I denied all accusations but I doubt anyone believed me but I really didn't care.

The next day, I rolled over and jumped up when I read the clock.

"Its 8:30! OMG! I overslept!" In a hurry, I rushed to get ready and sped all the way to work. Luckily my favorite co-worker Lindsay clocked me in and covered for me until I got there. When I got to my desk, I was overwhelmed because I was swamped with emails and phone calls and on top of that, my computer was moving at the pace of a snail! Because my morning was off to such a rocky start, I wasn't in the best of moods. I was so focused on my crap-load of work, I didn't even notice the seemingly rather agitated lady standing in front of my desk.

"I'm here to see Julius!" She said rudely.

"Excuse me ma'am?" I replied. "Do you have an appointment? Mr. Parker is in a meeting right now."

"I don't need an appointment, I'll just head to his office and when I get there, I'll be sure to let him know how long you kept me waiting and how you tried to hassle me about an appointment!" She scurried on towards his office in rage.

Baffled, I looked over at Lindsay. "Who's that nut cake, you seen her in here before?"

"Yes, of course." She replied. "That's Mrs. Hannah Parker, JULIUS' WIFE."

Chapter 4 - (intro)

I was so lost, I didn't know what to do.
You said you'd always be there,
Where were you when I really needed you?
I see now you really didn't care.
I've been betrayed.
Caught up in this lust, I've lost all trust.
Love for you is now delayed.
Searching for the truth, which I cannot find.
I'm trying to figure out what to do without you by my side.
Leaving all of our memories behind.
Just when our story was about to begin,
Here comes a tragic end.
I tried to hold on for goodness sake,
*We have made a.... **Beautiful Mistake***

Chapter 4

"Come on Naya, one more, you're almost there, PUUUSH!" I felt like I was dreaming, but those cries let me know that this was definitely my reality. I was officially the mother of the beautiful, six pound, two ounce Morgan Chanel Sutler. I couldn't believe she was finally here! This had been a long tedious eight and a half month journey and I'm looking forward to the future with my Princess.

I just pray that I am able to care for her and provide enough love for both mommy and daddy so she lacks nothing. Morgan's father left us the day I refused to abort her. His exact words when he purchased and handed me the test were and I quote, "If it's positive, you already know what to do!"

Blake and I had been together for three and a half years and we had our future planned to a T! I'm eighteen and just graduated high school and he's twenty-two and is currently working as a mechanic. The plan was when I finished high school, we were to move to Los Angeles. I applied and got accepted into one of the best colleges there were and I planned on obtaining a degree in psychology.

While I was attending school, he'd supposed to be focusing on his rap career. He had been saving for our future since the day we became official and he already had things lined up for our move which was ironically supposed to be next week. After we had accomplished everything we set out to do, we planned on getting married and having two kids, one girl and one boy. We literally had every step of our lives planned. First comes love, then comes marriage, then came Naya with the baby carriage. Isn't that how that old saying went?

Obviously things didn't go as planned. When I first found out I was pregnant, I convinced myself it was a false positive, but of course my Doctor visit proved me wrong. I wasn't ready to be a parent and according to our plans, it wasn't time yet. So yes, I scheduled an abortion, but the moment I heard my baby's heartbeat, I knew I could never go through with it. Blake accompanied me to the appointment but the beautiful heartbeat that seemed like the sound of music to my ears, had no effect on him at all. He still wanted to go through with it.

The ride on the way home from the doctor's office was pure silence. We arrived back at my house and that's when he broke up with me. I knew having a child would change things for us, but I had no idea it would tear us apart. I have not seen or spoken to Blake since that day. I tried calling him a few times but I got no answer. To my surprise, Blake came to the hospital the day after Morgan's birth. He didn't stay long and didn't even want to hold her. He claimed he was just dropping in to check on me because he heard I had my baby. Yes, he actually said "MY" baby and not "OUR baby." I guess he was right though, because she is *my* baby.

Before leaving, Blake told me he was still moving to California next week as planned and how he wished I could've came too. I wished him well and never saw him again.

* * * * * * *

Today was my baby girl's first birthday. It was so hard to believe that she was already one! What a crazy but wonderful year this had been. In this past year, I've completed my freshman year of college and I have also been working full-time as manager at a local coffee shop. It had not been easy juggling school, work and a busy baby but by the grace of God I have managed to make it through. I never would've guessed my life would turn out this way but believe it or not, I wouldn't have it any other way. I see now that you can still follow your dreams even if things don't go exactly as you planned. Though my baby came along with a lot of sacrifices, Morgan's the best thing that has ever happened to me. She has made me wiser, stronger, and so much better than I was before.

Growing up, I was spoiled and I had everything handed to me. I worked for nothing. Now, I worked for *everything* so that she wants for nothing. I've grown closer to God since Morgan's birth because besides her, He's all I have.

I moved out of my parent's house four months after giving birth. Don't get me wrong, they love Morgan, but they never let me forget what a *mistake* she was and a distraction to my future. My dad blamed Blake and my mom blamed me. My mom wanted me to focus more on Morgan than work, and my dad wanted me to focus on school. Neither of them believed I could juggle all three and when you're in someone else's house, you must follow their rules. So, since I didn't agree with them, I left. Since then, I've been completely on my own with just me and my Princess.

The evening crept up quick and I was supposed to be meeting with my parents and a few family members for Morgan's birthday. I was excited to see them and I'm sure they will be happy to see us as well.

Everyone was all happy and celebrating at the party, but for some reason, I was a little dampened. I really wished Blake was there to celebrate with us even though he hadn't seen her since she was two days old. He and Morgan were perfect strangers.

It would be nice for him to had been there. Sometimes I would sit and wonder what life would be like had he stuck around and what kind of father he would've been. I wondered if Morgan would've been a daddy's girl. What kind of family would we had been? Just thinking about it had me almost moved to tears.

"Naya, it's time for cake and candles!" My mom clapped, scaring me out of my daze. We all sung happy birthday, had cake and everyone went home. Judging by Morgan's smiley face and messy shirt, I think it's safe to say she enjoyed her day.

While cleaning up the mess from the party, my mom pulled me to the side.

"Blake called to wish Morgan a happy birthday. I'm surprised he even remembered her birthday. I gave him an update on how your life is right now including where you live, where you work, and even where you attended school. He told me that he got signed to some huge record label and he's finally living his dreams. He basically told me everything his mom told me when I saw her in the grocery store. She bragged about his new car and nice house."

I interrupted her. "Well that's good for him." I said.

My mom planted her hands on her hips. "Naya, you need to quit being stubborn and see if he is still single. I got his number." She cut her eyes at me.

I didn't even respond to her. Although I still loved him, I could care less about him and about what he had. Besides, if I were to call him, he'd swear it was only because I heard of his success, forgetting the fact that I am the mother of his daughter.

After putting Morgan to bed, I contemplated calling Blake. I called, hung up, drafted a text and erased it a thousand times. Finally I just typed up a text, closed my eyes and sent it.

It read: *Hey. My mom told me you called. Thank you for checking on us and for the B-day wish☺. Morgan really enjoyed her day. She's sound asleep right now! I wish you could've been here to celebrate with us but I'm sure you were busy. Hope all is well, congrats on everything!"* I then text him a picture of Morgan in her cute little pink tutu.

He replied quicker than I thought: *I'm good and I'm glad Morgan's good. Wow, she's looking just like her pops. Thanks for the well wishes, I'll see my daughter soon enough.*

I had no idea what he meant by seeing her soon.

I text him back: *Yeah, I hope so, she needs her father!*

He text back right away again: *Real soon, she'll have the family/life she's been missing. Reallll soon.*

I really hope he doesn't think his newfound fame will win my heart back because it won't. He left me when I needed him most, he abandoned not only me, but his daughter as well. Yes, I love him and yes, I want Morgan to have her dad in her life, but we don't have to be together to make that happen and I hope he knows that. I put my cell phone away and I said my prayers and went to sleep.

I was awakened by a loud knock at my door the next morning. I looked out of the window and saw a police car in my driveway. I ran to the door thinking it was some sort of emergency when I saw the Sheriff.

"Naya Sutler" he asked.

"That's me." I was confused.

"This is for you." He handed me a manila envelope.

I immediately breathed a sigh of relief because I was thinking the worst. I closed the door and when I got back to my room, I opened the envelope. In it was a bunch of papers stapled together. What caught my eye was the first page.

It read:

Naya Marie Sutler vs. Blake Lee Baxter
Defendant   Plaintiff
Summoned for court on: June 19
Type of Court: Probate

"The said Plaintiff has reason to believe that the defendant is unable to provide proper care to their shared child, therefore deemed unfit. The Plaintiff wishes to obtain full custody of said child proving he can provide better care. Both parties must attend a court hearing on date/time listed above to determine whether joint or full custody will be awarded to either party."

I thought to myself, *oh Blake, you never cease to amaze me, HA! You will NEVER get my daughter.*

Chapter 5 - (intro)

I played the fool when I should've known better,
When God is trying to tear something apart
You can't expect to keep it together.
They say love is war, well you better get your armor
You may need more than that to protect you from
A thing called.... **Karma**

Chapter 5

My husband hasn't been paying me any attention, so what else am I to do? Was I wrong for giving the guy at the gym my number? Should I have stopped him when he complimented me every day of the week? What about dinner? Should I not have taken him up on that offer? These are all thoughts that constantly raced through my mind now that things have gotten too deep.

At first it was supposed to be harmless fun, nothing more than a friendship. I mean, Chase knows that I'm married so we could never get too serious, and I love my husband but we're just going through a rough time right now. Chase is just someone I can talk to when I've had a long day. My husband Keith is a truck driver, so he's on the road a lot. He's never home for more than a day or two at a time.

When he's home, he's always tired from work and from driving all day. Either that or stressed out about work and wondering where his next load is coming from. His stress and complaining was starting to drain me. I honestly couldn't tell you the last time Keith and I had a date night. I don't even remember the last time we kissed. He's a good man, I can't deny him that. He goes above and beyond to make sure our bills are paid and that our son is taken care of. He also provided me the luxury of being a stay at home mom. Keith brings home the bacon and I cook it. I guess you could say, I'm a housewife.

Bags, cars, clothes, credit cards and shopping sprees. All of those things are nice but material things get old. Michael Kors and Christian Louboutin can't keep me warm at night and I can't cuddle with Fendi, Prada can't tell me everything's going to be okay, Dior can't teach our son to be a man and Versace can't make love to me. I really appreciate Keith and all that he does and I acknowledge his hard work, but we have to have balance. In his busy schedule, there has to be time for me. I'm not making excuses, I'm just saying. Mama always told me, "What one won't do, another will." I guess that's where Chase comes in.

It all started when I was leaving the gym one day and my car wouldn't start. I couldn't call Keith because he was on the road. I was about to panic because my son's game started in fifteen minutes and I couldn't stand to miss it. Chase came to the rescue and gave me a ride. While on the way to and from the game, that's when we got in depth and started to share more personal things with one another. Chase was once married but was now divorced. His wife wanted to find herself by traveling the world leaving Chase alone to raise their two daughters. That's where we connected. He's a single parent and you may as well say I am too since Keith is hardly home.

From then on, Chase and I started spending more time together outside of the gym. He came to all of my son's games and even took him to his practices. He was just there to motivate him whenever he needed it because Keith was never around. Chase and my son became really close, almost like he was his back-up father. Every moment Keith missed, Chase was there to see. In return, I did the same for his daughters. I helped with their hair, gave them advice and just spent a lot of girl time with them. Even when my husband Keith was around, I'd spend time with Chase's daughters. He had no problem with me being a motherly friend to them. Our son even told him how much fun he was having with Chase and Keith seemed to be okay with it.

After a while, he grew tired of our son telling him how much fun he'd been having with another man.

"Y'all spending too much time with that Chase dude." My husband snapped. "What is it with this dude? He playing daddy to our son, you playing mama to his daughters, is there something you want to tell me?" He asked.

I rolled my eyes. "Chase is a friend, you know that! We met at the gym where I go twice a week, he's a single man trying to raise two girls; I'm just helping him out, that's all." I stated firmly, though I was slightly agitated. "As for him playing daddy, I can't help it that you're never home!" I added.

Keith went on rambling about how he was out making an honest living to afford us a comfortable lifestyle. What I can't seem to get him to understand is that this *lifestyle* means nothing to me. He is so caught up in his work that he's letting his family slip through the cracks. Our argument got heated and because of that, this was another night of us going to bed mad. There was no talking, touching, loving or nothing. This was exactly why I got what I needed from Chase.

Keith and I had a long talk the next morning. We discussed everything that had been going on. He apologized on his behalf and I apologized on mine. He promised to try to be more present and I promised to be more understanding when he can't. Since we were turning a new leaf in our marriage, I decided to be totally honest about my slip-ups with Chase. Even though there was no justifying it, I also explained why I felt like I did what I did.

To my surprise, Keith was very forgiving, he was angry, but forgiving. I promised him that things between Chase and I were completely over. Now I just had to tell Chase. I can't lie, during the past few months, Chase and I have gotten very close. We've shared the most intimate parts of ourselves with one another. I never intended for things to go this far but sometimes shit just happened. The right thing to do was to break things off with Chase and work things out with my husband. I've seen so many failed marriages happen around me and I did not want to be a part of that statistic. Although Keith was hardly around, my son still loved his father.

Chase was a big distraction from my husband's absence, but there's nothing like the bond of a father and son. I want my family to work and in order for that to happen, all ties with Chase must be cut, TODAY.

I sent Chase a text telling him to meet me somewhere so we could talk and he agreed. He met me at the smoothie bar across from the gym. I sat him down and told him that whatever we had was over and I'm working things out with my husband.

"What? So you just gon' leave us too, huh? The girls and I just like Melissa did. You're just going to abandon us?!? I thought you cared for us, I thought you loved me?" He actually cried.

"Chase!" I pleaded. "I was in a vulnerable space, I never meant for this to be more than a friendship!"

The look on his face was as if I had shattered his world.

"You didn't love me!" He shouted.

"No I didn't, all of this was a mistake." I explained.

"A mistake, huh?" Chase repeated. His grin then turned into a smile. "Well that's news for me, now I got news for you...I'm HIV Positive!"

Chapter 6 - (intro)

I gotta' leave, I gotta' go.
I gotta' hide my feelings so they no longer show.
No matter how many tears I have to wipe away,
I've made up in my mind, I will not stay.
I'm no longer playing your silly little games,
*I'm...***Breaking the Chain**

Chapter 6

On the outside looking in, you'd think I was some foolish little girl for trying to hold on this long. What you don't know is, the love we've shared all these years. Through the ups and downs, truth and the lies, one thing remains the same, and that's real love on both ends. I now realize that nothing can change, alter, or erase the love one has for another and I do mean nothing. I sit and wonder why I can't leave when I have no business staying and the answer is love!

Jacob and I are going through a rough patch right now but I know everything will be alright. As soon as he gets another job everything will go back to normal. I keep telling him that doors will be opened for us soon enough. It's easy for me to think positive but Jacob is too much of a pessimist. After losing his job, it would be safe to say he lost his mind along with it. All he does is lay around the house, gripe and drink. Meanwhile, I'm picking up extra shifts at the diner to make ends meet.

After a long day of work, it'd be nice to come home to a home cooked meal, bath and a massage from my man. I would even settle for a, "Hey, how was your day?" Instead, all I get is a, "What's for dinner?" I don't ask for much, but a little help would be nice. Even though Jacob has more free time than me, I'm the one doing all the cooking, cleaning, etc. I know those are wifely duties, but the man is supposed to bring home the bacon or at least some of it. Whenever I try to talk to him about doing more, it just turns into a huge argument so I say nothing and do everything.

Since Jacob's recent unemployment, stress had been really weighing heavy on him. As his soon-to-be-wife, I know that I am supposed to be there for him through tough times and that is exactly what I have been trying to do. We have had plenty trying times throughout the years and we always managed to make it through. It wasn't easy, but we did make it through.

Jacob has always been the provider and work for me was literally just for fun. Now that I am the one *bringing home the bacon*, Jacob feels emasculated. Anything I say, he takes it as me talking down on him when it's usually just me trying to encourage him. I understand the masculine ego, but how can he sit around all day, mope and expect opportunities to come to him with no effort?

I finally told him how I felt about him being a couch potato all day and not seeking any employment. I also mentioned that the diner was hiring for bus boys.

"I am over qualified for a piece of shit job like that!" He snapped.

"Well you being qualified with no job, won't pay the bills." I replied sarcastically. Next thing I know, I'm pulling myself up off the floor. He quickly ran over to grab me apologizing for putting his hands on me. I was in total shock but I should've known before long my face would take place of the walls he used as his punching bags. Jacob has always had a slight problem with his anger, but he has never physically taken it out on me.

Lately, it seems like the Jacob I fell in love with has disappeared. I'm engaged to marry someone that I don't even know. I have never seen this side of him and I don't think I like it, nor do I think I can deal with it for the rest of my life. Vows are for better or for worse and I'm not sure I can make that agreement with him. I love him, true enough, and he says he's sorry, but I'm sure he's lying. He said he was sorry for the verbal abuse but it continues daily. He apologized for his ungrateful attitude but yet, he still has it. I never thought I was marrying a perfect person, but I never would've guessed he was an abusive one! I love Jacob, but I refuse to stick around for this. My mom told me stories of how my grandparents fought and I watched my uncle apologize to my aunt, only to pound on her again when he got mad. I've been awakened many nights from the screams in my mother's room, and have placed countless ice packs on my sister's blackened eyes.

I know how the game goes, therefore this cycle ends here! One time is already too many. My sister would cry to me all night and go back to her boyfriend the next morning. Then she'd be back next week with another scar and that just won't be me. She'd say, "He loves me, he's just going through a rough time right now!" I found myself justifying Jacob's irate behavior with those same words. It wasn't until my sister ended up fighting for her life in the hospital that she decided to leave her man alone for good. It won't take that much for me; Jacob's things will be waiting by the door when he wakes up in the morning!

Just as I expected, Jacob begged, pleaded, cried, lied and apologized over and over again. On his knees, like a sad puppy with crocodile tears, making their way down his cheeks. Paying him little to no attention, I went ahead and continued to get ready for work and asked that he and his things would be gone by the time my shift ended. Luckily for him, I have to work a double so he has more than enough time to move out.

I clocked out at exactly 9 pm and arrived home fifteen minutes later. To my surprise, Jacob's things were no longer at the door and the house was spotless. That was until I headed down the hallway where a trail of roses led right to my master bathroom. In the bathroom was a tub full of bubbles surrounded by candles. I don't know where he came from but when I turned around, Jacob was there on his knees yet again crying, begging, apologizing, and promising. Promising to be a better man, promising that more nights like tonight will await me after work, promising to try harder, do better, and most of all, promising to never hit me again. And just like that, the cycle continues.

Chapter 7 - (intro)

I'm sick and tired of being sick and tired!
It's like the more I pray, the harder it gets.
I take two steps forward only to be knocked ten steps back.
I've wept many nights..Where was my joy?
I believe things in the bible to be true,
So I'm waiting on my breakthrough.
In the meantime the bills are due.
I'm unsure where the money is coming from,
But I know where my help does.
I'm looking to the hills, but that ain't stopping my bills.
I've prayed the prayer of faith,
I don't know how much more I can take.
Mama says she knows what's blocking my blessings.
I told her it nothing more than the norm,
I'm just... **Weathering the Storm**

Chapter 7

I'm going through what seems to be the toughest time of my life. Just when I thought things were getting a little better, they start to get worse and right when I think things can't get any worse, they do. There is an old saying, *there's always someone wishing to be where you are.* If someone was wishing to step into my shoes, they must be insane!

Things were really going great for me at one point. I finished school, got a job, moved out of my mother's house and bought my own. I'd say I was doing pretty well for myself. I had it all together and somehow things just took a turn for the worse. I was head Accountant at my firm, working directly under the boss. All of my bills were paid and I was living the life, or so I thought.

It's true what they say, you can be up one minute and down the next. Seems like every day, things just started to fall apart. First, my company had budget cuts so my salary decreased making it nearly impossible to pay my eight-hundred dollar mortgage each month and still cater to my other expenses. Then, we lost funding as a whole and I lost my job. I was now jobless with an eight-hundred dollar mortgage, four hundred dollar car payment, and all other responsibilities that comes along with being an adult. As a result of that, I lost my home and had to move back in with my mother. Thankfully, she agreed to help with my car payments until I found another job. I'm almost thirty and back at square one. My plan was to lighten my mom's load not add to it.

Losing everything was definitely not a part of my five year plan. I won't stress too bad though, everything happens for a reason and I believe this was just a test that would make a great testimony one day.

An entire year has passed and I still found myself unemployed. Something's really got to give because my mom's been stressing that she can't continue to pay my car note. On top of that, bill collectors have been calling my phone day and night. I've already lost my job *and* my home, the least they could do was let me keep my car. I have always been a prayerful person and I've been praying extra hard lately.

Growing up, I stayed in the church's Sunday school every Sunday, Bible study every Wednesday, prayer meetings on Fridays and revivals every night of the week, when they are in season. My faith was always strong although I've been praying for a job for a whole year now and haven't had any luck.

I am starting to think I should take my friend Tori up on her offer. Tori dances at one of the hottest clubs in the city and brings home two to three thousand dollars in a single night sometimes. She said that she could talk to her boss and get me hired in no time. I thanked her but I declined her offer. Stripping goes against everything I believed in. Not to judge anybody, but that's just not my cup of tea. Plus, I've heard about the other things aside from dancing that goes on in strip clubs. I'd rather not have to result to that, but from the looks of it, I may have no choice.

The moment I lost my job, she offered to help to get me a job with her. I was so sure that something else would come through for me that I immediately declined. Now that it's been a year and nothing has changed, I decided to give Tori a call.

"Are you sure Elise?" She asked, knowing how against dancing I was. I assured her that I was one hundred percent sure and just like she promised, I was employed in no time.

"We can work as a team until you learn the ropes and loosen up a bit." Tori told me once it was official that I'd be one of her co-workers. I was glad of that because I was super nervous.

It was the first night of work and we were to be on in fifteen minutes. Tori suggested that it'd be a good idea to come up with a stage name. Hers was *Notorious* and at the very last minute I decided mine would be *Ego*. A blonde haired girl wearing a headset came in and told us we were up next. My anxiety took over and I instantly began to shake.

"Remember E, just like we practiced" Tori coached, in an attempt to calm my nerves. I took a deep breath and before I knew it, I was on stage dancing like a pro. Judging by the over-flow of dollar bills, I guess I was doing a pretty good job. I looked over at Tori and I thanked God she was with me because I don't know if I could've kept my vomit down without her.

After the show, I formally met the boss whose real name I didn't know because he preferred to be called *Boss*. Boss told me I did really well for the first time, but I needed to relax a bit more. He also told me that this duo Tori and I have formed was a good look, but for outside gigs only. Tori had *regulars* that would rather see her perform alone, so the next time I take the stage, I'd be dancing alone. Seeing the fear on my face, Boss told me not to worry because he had just the thing to help me relax.

All of my reservations on stripping had gone out the win-dow. A little over a month in the game and I was all in! I was loving the money that I was bringing home. I loved it so much so that I had saved up enough to move into an apartment.

Between dancing at the club and dancing at other gigs with Tori, I was almost back on my feet. My mother knew I worked at a club, but she thought I was bartending. If she knew what I really did, I'm almost positive she'd have a heart attack.

Tori was shocked at how much I had come out of my shell; she actually suggested that I should slow down a bit. Every ounce of nervousness went out the window with every puff of smoke that I inhaled. It's like I just closed my eyes and let the music take me away and before I knew it, I was literally dancing my life way.

I won't lie, the fast lane had really consumed me. Between dancing at the club every other night, to the outside gigs with Tori and my private shows with my regulars, I was in too deep. I never have time to rest and my mom was on my back because I've missed one too many Sunday services.

"Elise who in the world are you tending to at ten o'clock on a Sunday morning?" My mom asked with concern in her tone.

"You'd be surprised!" I answered.

"Well whomever it is, doesn't come before God! Sounds to me like ya' sleeping." She replied.

"Mom, I promise I'll be there next Sunday, front row and center." I hung up really hopeful. I was going to try my best to keep that promise because she was right, I need to be in church. Nothing comes before my time with God, definitely not dancing!

I decided to get up and go surprise my mother with a visit. I know she cooked some good Sunday dinner. As soon as I hit the doorstep I could smell the aroma from her kitchen. Homemade macaroni, fried pork chops, collard greens, cornbread, potato salad, sweet tea and a homemade peach cobbler alamode was for dessert. She cooked all of my favorites and didn't even know I was coming! Two of my aunts and uncles, Mrs. Hazel, my mom's friends from church and my nom were at the table about to say Grace when I entered. My mom jumped up so happy to see me that she fixed my plate in no time. I was really glad that

I came, it had been almost a month since I've seen my mom and an even longer time since I saw the others.

Dinner was lovely, the only problem now was that I was so full that I got sick. Mama had been telling me how exhausted I looked and demanded that I take a nap on the couch before leaving; especially since I felt sick. I told her that I had to get to work but she insisted that I stay. The only thing I remember from then was hugging everybody, saying goodbye and heading to the door. How I woke in a hospital room was beyond me. All I know is that now there was an IV in my arm, beeping machines all around me and an oxygen mask in my nose. I looked around the room puzzled and saw my mom at my side. For some reason I couldn't find any words to speak, all I could ask was, "What happened?"

"Look Elise, you collapsed at my door when you were heading out. The Doctor says you're suffering from extreme exhaustion and also found *cocaine* in your system. Care to explain?"

Chapter 8 (intro)

The pressures of life will have you so confused,
It's almost impossible to come out without a bruise.
Whether it be physically, mentally, financially, or emotionally,
Life has a way of making you lose your dignity.
Why it happens is a reason I can't see,
But God promised he wouldn't put more than I can bear on me.
So with my faith, I'm blocking all of these tackles,
I'm determined to loosen these.... **Shackles**

Chapter 8

Having been through what I've been through, it's nice to finally see a breakthrough. For the longest time, I've listened to people tell me, *it's going to get better* but I never saw a way. I was only focused on the right now, forgetting my faith. It's just something about having bill collectors knocking at your door, repo trucks in your driveway, negative numbers in your bank account, an empty wallet and friends who distance themselves from you that makes it hard to see the silver lining in any situation. I mean seriously, when everything seemed to be falling apart around me, how was I supposed to keep it together? After being knocked down as far as I could go, I couldn't see a way up. I'm just grateful that in the midst of it all, God didn't give up on me.

A few short days after graduation, I learned I was pregnant, and of course that came as a shock to me. I knew the minute I heard the baby's heartbeat, my life was over. I was hurt, confused and most of all disappointed. Though this kid was a total mistake, I knew my only option was to take care of my responsibility and raise him or her. I won't lie, it wasn't love at first sight because I saw him as more of a burden than a blessing. His father scolded me every day for refusing to care for him in any way. While I went through what I called postpartum and my mom called wrestling with the devil for the first six weeks of my son's life, my mom cared for him. She along with the help of my baby's father, Christopher. Christopher and my mom even named him. I regret being so resentful because they gave my boy a girl's name, Christian Faith. I cried when he was born and I cried every day for two months after we came home from the hospital.

The first month I cried because I didn't want him and the second month because I grew to love him and felt awful for not instantly loving him. I remember lying in bed crying as my mom attempted to pray away the spirits of resentment and depression. She would always rub my forehead with oil and whisper with her sweet voice, "Baby, this too shall pass."

I later discovered she was right. One day as my mom was feeding Christian, he began to cry non-stop. He wasn't wet, sleepy or anything but he was screaming to the top of his lungs! I reached for him and the very second she placed him in my arms, he stopped crying. I knew then that this little boy needed me! He didn't ask to be here and he didn't deserve the way I had been treating him. I remember hearing in my parenthood classes that babies could feel their mother's energy. My heart broke at the thought of my baby feeling as if his mommy didn't love him. I realized that to him, I am everything, and God gave him to me for a reason.

While my friends were packing, prepping and getting ready to leave for College, I was going back and forth to the doctor preparing to become a mommy. I was so miserable because things didn't go as I planned and I felt like a complete failure.

My dream was to be a nurse, but instead, I was flipping burgers and raising a baby.

The minute I thought life was sweet, it turned sour and as time went on, things got harder. I felt as though my world had been turned upside down in and instant. I went from happily married, to being better off divorced. From riding, to walking and from well enough to not enough. I went from thanking God for the opened doors, to questioning him for the missed opportunities.

I laid awake some nights wondering how my son and I would make it through the next day. I even contemplated suicide. Just when I felt like giving up, I heard my mom's sweet voice.

"Baby, this too shall pass." After hearing those words, I fell to my knees in prayer. I began to pray over my life, my son's life and against any spirit that tried to come amongst either one of us. I prayed myself to sleep and woke up feeling set free.

Now here we are, eight years later and I couldn't imagine life without my Prince! I have sacrificed a lot to ensure Christian's wellbeing but I wouldn't trade it for the world! He's so smart and excels in all that he does. He's a momma's boy and I love it! Though I'm not happy with the detour my life took, I know that everything happens for a reason. The little boy I thought was a burden, turned out to be my biggest blessing yet! God knew exactly what he was doing when he gave me Christian. When I look at him, I'm reminded of the lesson I was taught.

Life is full of surprises. Good, bad, and ugly. You just have to roll with the punches and remember not to throw in the towel! Sometimes detours will take you right where you need to go. You must trust the journey that God is leading you on and know that delays are not denials. Even when your burdens get heavy and everything seems to be going wrong, you have to trust God to lighten your load and thank him for things being as well as they are.

My son to me is an assurance of God's grace and I don't think it was just a coincidence that my mom named him, *Christian Faith.*

Chapter 9 - (intro)

In life you lose.
In life you gain.
In life at times you feel nothing but pain.
In life you laugh,
In life you cry.
In life sometimes you feel like you can't even try.
But;
No matter what happens today, no matter what life throws my way,
I'm carrying burdens no
longer.
Now that I've laid them down, I'm so much.... ***Stronger***

Chapter 9

I would always see homeless people on the street and wonder how they ended up there. It wasn't until I became one myself that I found the answer to that question. At the tender age of sixteen, I had to learn to fend for myself. Daddy wasn't present, grandma was gone, and momma didn't care about anything other than *her* man. It all started when I told momma that Robby, the man she loved so much, made me feel uncomfortable. I told her that he touched me in ways that made me hurt. Momma slapped me, called me a liar, and packed my clothes. I hit the streets and haven't seen momma since.

The streets became my best friend and my worst enemy. It was the place I called home and the place where everyone and everything seemed to be out to get me. It was where I found my first love and my first hustle. You'd be surprised how many teenagers there were out there all alone like myself.

While spending hours inside of the twenty-four hour waffle house wondering what my next move would be, I met an eighteen-year-old girl named Bri. Like me, she was kicked out of her home with nowhere else left to go. She too spent hours in the waffle house contemplating her next move, fidgeting in her seat like me. I think that's part of the reason she could tell I wasn't there willingly. Well, that and my bags of course.

After sharing stories, we realized we had a lot in common.

Bri then took me to this old abandoned building that used to be a Laundromat. It was where she and many other homeless teens lived. Inside were worn mattresses and pallets along the walls. They had a few lanterns lit which were used for light and to my surprise, they actually had running water in the restroom's sink and the toilet worked. They used the old washing machines as cabinets to store their food, which were mostly canned goods and there were about ten of them staying there. They seemed to have formed some sort of family. They shared everything: clothes, shoes, food, etc. Some of them actually had jobs but weren't quite making enough to move out just yet. Bri introduced me to everyone and they were actually quite welcoming. They offered me food and blankets. I was actually kind of intrigued to see how they were making the best out of what they had. Everyone was like one big happy family living in a Laundromat instead of a house.

That night I shared Bri's pallet. When I woke up the next morning, I felt as though I was being awakened from a nightmare which turned out to be my new reality. I was the first one up, it seemed. I observed my surroundings in the daylight and realized that yes, this was now my life and I began to cry. Tears were flowing down my cheeks like a river. I tried not to let out a loud cry for fear of waking up Bri or someone else. Turns out I wasn't the only one up. Just as I began to sniffle, the bathroom door opened. Out walked Christophe, an eighteen year old male resident of the Laundromat. It looked as if he was getting ready for work, judging by his McDonald's uniform. He handed me some tissue and offered to make me breakfast, which was only a can of beans and a bottle of water. Unlike me, Christophe was not kicked out, he ran away because of abuse. His parents moved here from New Mexico so he had no other family in the area. Christophe said he'd been staying in the Laundromat since he was sixteen and hasn't seen or spoken to his parents since. I really felt for him because even though my momma chose to put Robby before me, she's all I have as far as family and I couldn't imagine never seeing or talking to her again.

It had been two and a half years since Christophe had any contact with his family, and at this very moment, they hadn't the slightest idea of knowing if he was dead or alive and vice-versa. The mere thought of that becoming my reality brought me to tears. Christophe of course attempted to comfort me and assured me that things weren't that bad.

He told me that although he misses his parents, he has found family right here at the Laundromat. He even revealed that he felt more safe, secure, and loved. More than he ever had at home. He said that he's been employed for almost a year and has been saving to get an apartment.

After sharing my story and telling him that I see absolutely no way to find even a spec of joy in that, Christophe looked me in the eyes.

"Sometimes when you don't see a way out, you have to make one!" He smiled, squeezed my hand and then he left for work.

"Making friends already I see." Bri said in a sleepy tone.

I smiled, "I guess so." I said.

After finishing my beans, I washed up and brushed my teeth in the restroom sink. All I could do was cry. I just couldn't believe this was really happening. Things I've watched on TV and read in books have become real life for me. I cried like that for a full three weeks straight. I asked Bri if the tears would ever stop and she assured me that they would eventually. She said that I'd become accustomed to it just like the rest of them. Of course that too brought on the waterworks.

Accepting this reality was the hardest thing ever for me. Christophe often tried to cheer me up by assuring me it wouldn't be this way forever. I always thanked God for allowing Bri to take me under her wing and for Christophe for encouraging me, and the rest at the Laundromat's members for being so welcoming.

Each day we had breakfast, dinner and prayer service together. The prayer service thing was something I started. One of the younger teens there approached me with the saddest eyes.

"If you have so much faith and believe in the power of God, then why are you always crying? And if he's as good as you say he is, then how did you or any of us end up here?" I could tell she didn't ask me to be rude or malicious because she looked very curious. In that moment I stood convicted, because she was right. *Why was I crying all the time? Why couldn't I trust and believe that my right now won't be my forever?* I tuned back into the young girl who was awaiting an answer. I assured her that if we prayed sincerely and if we truly believed with all of our hearts, that God would hear us, then our prayers would be answered. I explained to her that sometimes God takes us through things just to see if we really trust him like we say we do. Then I told her that this is where our faith came in. Good or bad, God is with us and in due time he will deliver us.

By preaching to her, I discovered that I was actually preaching to myself in the process.

From that moment on, I didn't shed another tear about my current situation. Instead, I made the best out of it and started to look at the bright side of things. At least I wasn't living under a bridge or laying outside somewhere cold, alone and hungry. At the Laundromat I had, food, shelter and new friends who were starting to feel like family. After about three months in the Laundromat, it started to feel like home for me. It was almost like I started a new life. I had a supply of canned goods and water for breakfast every morning and sometimes the same for dinner. Christophe would also often bring us leftovers from work.

My living situation was a really humbling experience. I'd never eaten the same things every day when I lived with my mom and certainly not any leftovers. Over time, Bri and I had become the best of friends and Christophe and I had become really close as well. Bri would always joke and tell me how Christophe liked me. She even bet that one day I'd be his girl-friend and that we'd have some beautiful God babies for her with pretty hair.

A month later Christophe announced to everyone that he had saved up enough money and was finally moving into that apartment that he had been talking about. That moment was a bittersweet one for all of us. Especially the ones who had been there since the very first day that Christophe started staying there; which was nearly three years ago. After breaking the news about his apartment, Christophe then told everyone that he had another very special announcement to make. He got down on one knee and asked me to be his wife and of course I said, "YES!"

Chapter 10 - (intro)

Everything that glitters ain't gold.
That's always been a saying of the old.
Never judge a book by its cover, I was always told.
Those are true sayings, however; everyone won't agree.
Instead of searching for facts, they'd rather think discriminatory.
I'll leave them questioning logistics,
Wondering how I made it... ***Despite the Statistics***

Chapter 10

I've seen a lot during my time here on earth. I've lost people who meant the world to me and I've also watched the one I love, love someone else. I have watched my family bicker and fall apart over nonsense and I've once felt like an outcast in my very own home.

I felt like I had given my all to someone I know didn't deserve it and I've even climbed mountains for people who wouldn't even climb steps for me. I gave my heart away and loved wholeheartedly and I never felt loved in returned. There were a lot of things I set out to do that just didn't happen for me. I shot for the stars and didn't even reach the clouds.

As I got older, I realized obstacles can only hold you back if you allow them to.

Since birth, the odds were against me. I wasn't expected to live and if I lived I wasn't expected to walk, talk, eat or even breathe on my own. Growing up I was a spoiled brat, there was nothing as a child that I remember asking for and not receiving. I would ask for something and in no time it was in my hand. If it were possible, I probably could've had the world handed to me on a silver platter.

I was wise beyond my years so I rarely played with toys or dolls. I liked things like books, music, CDs, CD Players, movies, nail polish, organizers, EZ-Bake ovens and computers.

Although, I did like baby dolls, I liked to play mommy and be the boss! No lie, I remember being ten years old and asked by my elders to borrow money.

When I got a little older and started school, I always had nice clothes, shoes and kept a fresh hair-do. If ever there was a time that I wasn't snatched, it was because I didn't want to be. Things like that never really mattered to me. I mean, yes as a child it was always fun to gloat and compare toys with friends, but as I said, I was wise beyond my years so it was mostly to show off, not for play time.

From the outside looking in, you'd think I was living the life. What more could I ask for if I could have everything I wanted? Though I had everything, it didn't make life any easier for me. I faced many challenges in my life and material things just could not compensate for it. I had three different surgeries in the same spots, all of which began when I was about three or four years old and ended when I was nine. I spent a lot of my childhood in really uncomfortable casts. I was walking with a walker by the age of five and using crutches at ten. I started physical therapy when I was two and made a decision on my own to stop at fourteen. When most kids were wishing for toys on Christmas, I was begging my mother not to make me wear my braces. I've always tried to be as independent as possible and it always took a lot for me to accept help in any form from anybody because I like to show them I can do it on my own.

I spent my whole life listening to people tell me what I can and can't do. I made it my business to prove them wrong. Regardless of what seemed like a limitation, I knew there was nothing I couldn't do. I never gave my family, friends, teachers or anyone the room to treat me differently from anyone else. I took regular classes and attended all other functions that sparked my interest.

In my eyes, I'm just as normal as anybody else and capable

of doing whatever I wanted to do. Upon graduating high school, I set out to do other things that didn't quite go as planned. I made two attempts to go away to College and though I was accepted, I let the concerns of others keep me from going. I was a little bummed at first about not following my original plan, but I accepted it.

After getting over what felt like defeat, I started to get my mojo back and decided to attend online school, which was a very overwhelming experience. Before entering into summer semester, I let my laziness get a hold of me and decided to take a break. During that break I began to think, reflect and also realize that it had been two years since I had graduated from high school. I then thought to myself, *what have I done with my life these past two years? Have I accomplished anything? Am I really where I want to be?* That same day I shared those questions with a friend of mine.

"If you are not where you want to be, it's all *your* fault. You sit and plan things, but never follow through with them."

All I could do was swallow his words because he was right. He then reminded me of my vision of wanting to be a pediatrician and also reminded me that I changed my mind and wanted to be an ultrasound technician. He was right. I even changed my mind after that and wanted to be a psychologist, then an author. At one time, I even enrolled myself in College to study Radiologic Technology which has never been on my list!

I'm not sure if my friend knew it, but he gave me a reality check. I finally made up my mind that I would get serious about my writing. I actually started working on my book years ago and I had it all planned out. I made the mistake of telling people about it too soon. When I told them how I wanted to write a book, become an author, create my own publishing company and do the same for others, they laughed at me. They told me to be realistic and even though I knew better, I let them discourage me. Little did they know, this was not something I just woke up one morning and decided to do; it was something that I was really passionate about.

Writing has always been like therapy to me. Even as a child and still to this day, I keep a journal to vent and escape to my happy place. Maybe they should've been more realistic, because, guess what? You just finished reading a book that I wrote and published!